BATTLE BUGS

THE KOMODO CONFLICT

BATTLE BUGS

THE KOMODO *CONFLICT*

by **JACK PATTON**

illustrated by **BRETT BEAN**

SCHOLASTIC INC.

With special thanks to Adrian Bott

ISBN 978-0-545-79148-9

10 9 8 7 6 5 4 3 2   16 17 18 19 20

Printed in the U.S.A.   40
First printing 2016
Book design by Phil Falco and Ellen Duda

CONTENTS

CALL FOR HELP

Vacation was so close, Max Darwin could almost taste it. Soon, there would be no more classes and no more books! Now there was only one thing standing between him and bug-hunting fun in the sun: the school science fair.

The school gym was crowded with tables, each one showing off a different student's project. Letters made of colored paper and foil spelled out their titles.

Max and his friend Steve wandered up and down the rows of tables, checking out the competition.

"That potato battery is so lame." Steve laughed. "Come up with something original!"

"Like your soda volcano?" Max teased.

"Hey! The soda volcano is a classic. Like the Harley-Davidson."

Max rolled his eyes. "Whatever you say, Steve."

Max didn't think his friend had much chance of winning. He'd chosen his volcano project because it was easy and both his brothers had done it before him. Max, on the other hand, had worked hard on his own exhibit: a spectacular ant farm.

Max hoped he had a chance of making the top three. Although, he had to admit, some of the other projects were cool. One girl had made a rotating model of the solar system, and just across from his table, one boy had made a balloon-powered rocket.

The two boys crossed the gym and made it to Steve's workstation just as Principal Marsh did. Principal Marsh was tall and dressed all in brown, reminding Max of a walking stick bug.

"What's your project all about, Steven?" he asked.

Steve pointed proudly to the papier-mâché volcano he'd made. "I think it's better if I just show you."

The principal frowned, then shrugged. "Okay then." He tapped his pen on his clipboard, ready to take notes.

The kids from Max's class gathered around. They all seemed curious about what would happen.

"Whatever you have planned is certainly drawing a crowd," the principal said.

Max winked and passed Steve the all-important roll of Mentos. The volcano hid a big bottle of soda, and the crater at the top was the hole in the bottle.

"In ancient Pompeii," Steve began, "the citizens lived at the foot of Mount Vesuvius, going about their daily lives. Little did they know that the mountain held a secret. Vesuvius was no ordinary mountain: It was a volcano, and it was about to ERUPT . . ."

Steve reached across to the top of the model and dropped a whole fistful of Mentos into the crater. Max ducked for cover as the principal leaned in for a closer look.

WHOOMPSH! A foamy, brown geyser exploded out the top of the volcano. It blasted into the air, fizzing wildly, splashing the principal right in the face. His glasses flew off and he was drenched completely.

"Blarghhh!" he cried. Screams and squeals of surprise rang out, followed by laughter and cheers.

Steve grinned. ". . . And with that, Pompeii was buried for a thousand years."

Max looked at what was left of Steve's volcano. The force of the eruption had blown the mountain apart, cracking off a huge chunk of papier-mâché.

The principal picked up his glasses and wiped them with a handkerchief. "I should have known better than to get too close to the lava flow," he said, drily.

"Sorry, Principal Marsh," Steve said innocently. "I didn't know it would work so well."

"Let's just move on to the next project," Principal Marsh suggested. "Max. What did you make?"

Max led the principal across the gym to his table. The ant farm was a large glass-fronted box filled with dirt. Inside, ants happily tunneled around. Along the top of the box ran Max's project heading: THE WORLD OF ANTS.

He grinned as he read the words. *If I'd wanted to, I could have just paid a visit to Bug Island and visited the* real *World of Ants.*

The principal seemed impressed. "Excellent! Tell me more about it."

"I set the ants up with a lot of different foods to choose from, to see what they like best," Max explained. "Every day I observed them for an hour and wrote down how many

ants I saw eating each kind of food." He pointed at the chart he'd prepared. He knew one thing for sure now: Ants were crazy about sweet things.

The principal made a mark on his clipboard. "Very good. Fascinating little creatures, ants. In fact, there goes one of them now. Can I have a closer look?"

"Sure! I've got a magnifying glass you can use, right here."

Max reached into his pocket to pull out the magnifying glass, but instead he found the screwdriver he'd been using to build the ant farm. "Oops," he said. "Must be in my bag. Hold on."

He ducked under the table to grab his

backpack and then reached into it, trying to find the magnifying glass.

"Ow!" he cried, leaping back from his bag. His hand had touched something *hot*.

The principal raised an eyebrow in his direction but Max coughed weakly, trying to hide his alarm. *What was that?*

Carefully, he opened up his bag and felt for the hot thing again. It was almost painful to the touch, like laying your hand on a radiator that's been turned up too high. He felt the leathery cover and the rough edges of the pages, and that was when he knew.

It was *The Complete Encyclopedia of Arthropods*, the mysterious book that was the gateway to Bug Island. Every time the bugs needed help, the book glowed—but it had never been burning hot before.

There was only one explanation. This must be an emergency. The bugs were in real trouble.

Max snatched up his backpack and made his excuses. "Sorry, Principal Marsh, I guess I must have left my magnifying glass in the classroom. I'll be right back."

He stampeded through empty, echoing corridors, past the main office, and around the corner to his classroom. He poked his head in through the doorway.

It's empty! he thought. *Perfect!*

Max carefully closed the door behind him and pulled out the encyclopedia. It even *smelled* hot now, and the pages were glowing red.

He opened the book and flicked through the pages until he found the map of Bug Island. He grabbed the magnifying glass that was embedded in the cover and held it up over the page. Suddenly, a powerful force whirled around him like a tornado. Before he knew it, he was wrenched off his feet and sent tumbling straight into the pages of the book.

"Bug Island, here I come!"

UNWELCOME VISITOR

Max fell out of the sky and landed with a bump on soft sand. He got to his feet and saw he was standing on a dune, not far from the edge of the jungle. It was a bright, warm day, but there was no time to relax in the sun. He had to find his bug friends, and fast.

Max brushed himself off and scrambled to the top of the dune for a better view. He looked out across the beach and then over the bay toward Reptile Island, the home of the enemy.

In the distance, huge clouds of black smoke billowed out of the volcano at the heart of the island. The lizards called it the "Great Reptilicus," as if it were some kind of powerful monster. Right now, Max could understand why. The sky over the lizards' home was dark, menacing, and filled with smoke. The clouds directly above the volcano glowed red from the boiling lava inside.

It really is hot on the island this time, Max thought. Sweat ran down his face. *No wonder the encyclopedia felt like it was burning up.*

Suddenly, a buzzing noise overhead caught his attention. He looked up and grinned to see a familiar black-and-yellow shape diving down toward him.

"Buzz!" he cried.

Buzz, the giant hornet flight commander, waved a foreleg to say hello. "Max! I was on patrol and saw you fall out of the sky," she said. "You're here not a moment too soon. You'd better climb on board right away." Buzz's voice sounded much graver than usual.

"What's the hurry?" Max asked.

"General Barton has called a council meeting. He'll explain everything. Hop on."

Max clambered onto Buzz's prickly back. He couldn't believe his luck. For once, he'd crash-landed near the bugs, instead of miles away from them or stuck in a swamp somewhere.

Buzz flew over the sandy beach and through the jungle trees at breakneck speed. Max wanted to ask her what the big emergency was, but the roar of her wings was so loud he couldn't hear himself speak.

Soon they'd dodged the bright jungle foliage and come out into a wide clearing. Before they'd even landed, Max spotted the huge shape of Barton the titan beetle, leader of the Battle Bugs. He was perched on top of a muddy hill in the middle of the bug camp, with the bug army surrounding him.

Buzz made a high-speed landing in front

of Barton. Her legs skidded to a stop, churning up the mud.

"I found him, sir. Safe and sound." She saluted Barton.

"Excellent," Barton boomed in his deep, commanding voice. "Welcome back to Bug Island, Max."

Spike the emperor scorpion and Webster the trap-door spider stood on either side of Barton. They looked at Max anxiously.

"We need you more than ever, buddy," Spike said.

"Things have gotten real b-b-bad," Webster stammered.

Seeing the bugs so worried made Max feel uneasy. "What's General Komodo up to now?"

"It's not just one thing, Max. That's the problem," Barton rumbled. "As you know, we've suffered from lizard attacks ever since the volcano erupted and created the lava bridge. But lately, the attacks have become worse. Day and night they hammer away at us. They just aren't letting up!"

"What about your usual defenses?" Max asked. "You've always been able to slow the lizards down before."

Barton lowered his voice to a whisper. "That's the problem, Max. They don't seem to be working. It's as if the lizards know just what we're going to do."

"That *is* bad," Max said, feeling a chill spread over him. He tried to think of some reptile ability he might have read about that could explain it, but nothing came to mind. It sounded as if General Komodo was one step ahead of the bugs' forces.

"A-ha!" Barton boomed, seeing two other bugs approach. "Here come the new division commanders. Max, I'd like you to meet the head of offense, Jet. And this is Scuttler, head of defense."

Both Jet and Scuttler were impressive to look at, but for very different reasons. Jet was a spindly-legged black widow spider, as black and shiny as the stone she was named after. Scuttler was a bright metallic scarab beetle. His wing case gleamed green and gold.

"It's nice to meet you both." Max said. "Do you know some people back in my

world used to think scarab beetles were sacred?" he asked Scuttler.

"How strange," the beetle said. "Over here in Barton's army, I'm just a humble bug."

Scuttler's flashy wing case glinted in the sun. He didn't strike Max as the most humble of bugs. However, Max soon pushed the thought to the back of his mind.

"Let's get to work—" he began.

Suddenly, Jet scuttled forward blindingly fast, making Max yelp and leap backward in shock.

"You're no bug," she snapped, towering over him. Her legs looked like the sleek metal bars of a prison cage.

"No," Max gasped. "I'm human."

"Human? Never heard of it." She peered closely at him, her many eyes glittering with suspicion. "Why are you so nervous? Do you have something to hide?"

Max tried to form an answer, but the venomous black widow was terrifying. He thought all the bugs were supposed to be on the same side.

Scuttler came to Max's defense. "Jet, Max is General Barton's special adviser."

"Special adviser?" the spider sneered. "A likely story! He's not a bug, and in my book, that makes him a threat to Bug Island!" She swiveled her eyes back to Max. "I've got my eyes on you," she muttered, and backed away, still glaring at him.

"That will do, Jet!" Barton roared. "I

trust him, and that will have to be enough for you!"

Max was almost as shaken by Barton's anger as he had been by Jet's suspicion. It wasn't like Barton to lose his temper with one of his bug officers. Were the bugs really so frightened that they were turning on one another now? If so, Max thought, they needed him more than ever.

Barton called the meeting to order. "We need to decide what to do about the new lizard offensive. Max, any ideas?"

Max was still feeling uneasy after the confrontation with Jet, but he tried to calm down and think clearly.

"I guess the most important thing is to keep you safe, Barton," he said. "You're the leader, so you've got to be Komodo's biggest target."

"That makes sense," Spike agreed.

"In fact, all the commanders should stay here in the camp for now. You should be safe here. We've got the trip wires to warn us if the lizards try an attack." Max had set up an alarm system on one of his previous visits. It was made from spiderweb trip wires rigged to noisy, rattling acorn shells.

"You sound very confident," Jet said. "Are you *sure*?"

"Trust me. I set the trip wires up myself. There's no way any reptile could sneak through them . . ."

His voice died away. Suddenly, a shadowy form loomed at the far edge of the bugs' camp.

Scuttler saw it, too. "Defense stations!" he yelled.

The oncoming creature came into full sight. It was a huge lizard, ten times the length of Barton, covered in black and orange scales like the camouflage on an army tank. It moved with a slow, lumbering swagger, showing no fear at all. It flicked its tongue out and sniffed the air, then looked right at Max.

"Uh-oh," Max said. He knew exactly what the black-and-orange beast was. He also knew that it had venomous spit and an incredible sense of smell. If the lizard bit any of them, they were doomed.

"It's a Gila monster!" he shouted.

"Thought you were safe here, did you?" the lizard said, its mouth twisting into an evil grin. "Apparently, you were wrong!"

The ground trembled beneath Max's feet as the colossal reptile charged straight at him!

DEFEND THE HUMAN!

The Gila monster ignored all the beetles, mantises, and army ants that were surrounding the bug commanders. It stormed through them, scattering them to the left and right as if they were too small for it to bother with. The beast had Max in its sights, and Max knew it.

He knew one other thing, too. Gila monsters preferred to eat small animals rather than insects. Right now, he *was* a small animal. There was nothing left between him and it, apart from a low wall made from mud and fragments of vegetation.

"Close ranks!" Barton bellowed. "Defend the human!"

"Why is it coming for *me*?" Max yelled.

"I don't know, but right now we've got to keep you safe!" Barton answered.

One of the beetles in the lizard's way opened its wing case and flew out to meet the creature in battle. It buzzed up into the air just in front of the reptile's face—a big mistake.

The Gila monster's chomping jaws seized the helpless insect and flung it to one side.

Max stared at the fallen beetle. "Watch out! This reptile has venomous spit. Don't get any on you!"

The huge lizard climbed up and over the mud wall and bore down on Max. Luckily, although it was big, it was quite slow moving for a reptile. Max dodged quickly out of its path. The Gila monster's jaws slammed shut on thin air. Max ducked and rolled, careful to avoid any flying drops of poisonous spittle raining down around him.

Although they had at first been taken by surprise, the bugs were rallying. From all across the camp, warrior bugs piled in to

assault the reptile. Sharp mandibles bit and claws snapped, gouging at the creature's hide.

Max backed away and bumped into Scuttler. The insect looked like he was keeping well out of the way of the fighting.

"Aren't you going to attack it?" Max demanded.

"They don't need me at the front," Scuttler said. "I'm much more useful strategizing behind the scenes. Excuse me, I need to go and advise the bombardier beetles!"

As Max watched Scuttler go, he reminded himself that defense was just as much about preparing traps and barricades as it was about fighting. Not that those defenses would do them any good right now. The Gila monster was right in the heart of the camp, crushing the bugs' structures and collapsing burrows under its weight. What they needed was a swift counterattack.

"Spike!" he yelled to his scorpion pal. "Let's show this lizard what real venom's all about!"

"Now you're talking," Spike cheered.

The scorpion powered over to Max, who jumped swiftly onto his back. Together they charged forward. Spike clawed with his pincers and jabbed with his tail, while Max pointed out the soft parts of the Gila monster's body, where a strike would hurt most.

"We have to stop it," Max cried. "It's destroying the camp!"

Spike landed some good hits, making the monster lizard roar and groan in pain. But no matter what they did, they couldn't stop its rampage. The stockades and towers the termites had carefully built came crashing down around them. Bugs ran around buzzing and chirping in total panic.

Then, from out of the ranks, Jet the black widow came sprinting. "Enough of this!" she snarled. "Spider squadron, engage the enemy. Capture him alive!"

Max stared in amazement. In answer to Jet's call, hundreds and hundreds of spiders came scuttling out of the undergrowth. They glided down from the trees on silk lines like paratroopers, and some even leaped from the undergrowth, as agile as grasshoppers.

The spiders began to scramble up the Gila monster's body. At first it clawed them off, grunting in annoyance.

"What are you going to do, tickle me to death?" it grumbled.

But soon there were more spiders than it could deal with. Like a living carpet, they covered the startled reptile, completely enclosing it from snout to tail.

"Deploy webs!" Jet commanded.

The Gila monster struggled as the massive spider army began to wrap him in webbing. Its strength was useless against so many. No sooner had it broken one webbing line than a dozen replaced it.

The spiders worked quickly and silently. Before long, Max couldn't make out the black-and-orange pattern on the lizard's body anymore. He looked on with horrified fascination as they turned it into a living reptile mummy.

Eventually there was only a silvery cocoon with the Gila monster's head sticking out the top. The spiders hoisted it up in the air from a branch. Max remembered reading that spider silk could hold five times more weight for its size than steel.

"Permission to interrogate the prisoner, sir," Jet asked Barton.

"Granted," Barton replied.

Jet clambered up the Gila monster's swaddled body.

"I want answers!" she demanded. "What's going on in the lizard ranks?"

The lizard laughed. "It's all over for you bugs. Komodo's ordered an all-out assault on Bug Island."

"Why now?"

"To clear the way for us to move here, of course! You still don't understand, do you? The elder turtles have told us the Great Reptilicus is about to erupt tomorrow. We're evacuating Reptile Island for good."

Murmurs swept through the bug ranks.

"This army you're sending," Jet demanded, "how big is it?"

The Gila monster laughed even harder this time. "It's not just the lizard army that's coming, it's *every reptile* on Reptile Island!"

Still laughing, the reptile forced a final feat of strength. The webbing prison bulged and strained, then one of its claws broke free. "And there's nothing you can do about it!" He hissed in delight.

Jet yelled for the spider squadron, but the Gila monster was already pulling itself out of the torn webbing sack. It fell with a *whump*, shook itself groggily, and dashed off into the undergrowth.

"Buzz!" Max shouted. "Follow that lizard!"

"Roger that, Max," Buzz said, dashing off in pursuit.

An eerie silence hung over the shattered bug camp. Some of the fortress was still standing, but the Gila monster had done a lot of damage.

"Why didn't we see this coming?" Barton said.

"We were *supposed* to have an early warning system," Jet hissed. "Looks like your trip wires didn't work, human!"

"I'm sorry," Max said, confused. "They've always worked perfectly before."

He racked his brains to think of what might have gone wrong. How could something the size of a Gila monster have come so close without triggering a *single one* of his trip wires?

Jet glared at him, her eyes full of suspicion, and he could guess why. The lethal black widow must have thought he was a fool . . . or worse, a traitor.

Barton climbed to the top of a ruined termite tower. "One thing's for sure, my fellow bugs," he said darkly. "We've faced challenges before, but not like this. If every single reptile on Reptile Island is headed here, then this will be the biggest battle we've ever faced. The fate of Bug Island is hanging in the balance!"

THE WALL

Max looked at the worried bugs all around him. It was up to him to use his big human brain and help them out.

"Okay, guys, listen up!" he yelled, a plan already whirring through his mind. "The volcano is erupting tomorrow, so we've only got tonight to prepare our defenses. When they invade, the lizards are going to come across the lava bridge, right?"

"They have to," Barton said. "There's still no other way they could bring so many of their number to our shores."

"So we need to fortify the beaches," Max said. "C'mon. I'm gonna need termites, wasps, hornets, and all the bugs you can spare. We're building a wall!"

The bugs trooped through the jungle and headed down to the sandy beach. Buzz flew back to rejoin the group. "I lost sight of the Gila monster in the undergrowth," she told Max. "He seems to have injured his leg in the fall from the tree. He won't be back anytime soon."

"Join us on the beach," Max said. "I know you're our best flyer, but I need your squadron's nest-building skills for once."

"*Nest-building?*" Buzz repeated to herself, confused.

Max climbed to the top of a dune and looked out over the sea. The lava bridge to Reptile Island lay before him. The volcano was still belching black smoke.

The bug camp might have been in ruins, but at least the watchtower was still standing, up on the cliff above the beach. The termites had built it from mud, dung, and leaves so that they could watch the lava bridge for approaching lizards. They'd need it more than ever in the hours to come.

"We're going to build a wall across this beach as a first line of defense. You bugs are going to need to work together like never before," Max told them. "Here's the plan . . ."

With Scuttler acting as foreman, Max organized the bugs. They had a big wall to build, and precious little time to do it.

First, they needed building materials. The termites couldn't work with dry sand, so they needed a constant supply of mud and vegetation. That was where the ants came in. Since the ants were hard workers who could shift surprisingly huge loads, they were ideal supply bugs—and just as quick as the ones in Max's science fair project.

The ants formed themselves into a living chain, ferrying materials across from the jungle to the construction site. Within minutes of Max giving the order, little heaps of earth and debris were already starting to form along the beach.

"Great work!" chirped the termite leader.

Max clapped his hands briskly. "Now we need some wood for the wasps and hornets to chew up. Dobs?"

"HERE!" Dobs, the giant dobsonfly, boomed.

"I need you and the other dobsonflies to go get plenty of twigs and bark, so the nest builders don't have to keep flying back to the jungle."

"WE'RE ON IT!"

"Cool. Okay, termites: I need pillars here, here, and here. Hornets: Once the wood gets here, you fill up the space between with nest material."

After he'd given all the orders, Max sat down exhaustedly to watch his plans unfold. He'd done all he could. Now it was up to the bugs.

The bugs worked like crazy, fetching, carrying, chewing, and pasting. Termites squished together lumps of dirt, mixing it with gluey saliva to make stuff like clay to build with. Ants and dobsonflies kept the supplies coming. Buzz and her team of hornets chewed wood into pulp, building papery nests between the sturdy termite mounds. Alongside her, wasps did the same.

Spike came trotting across to him, along with Webster and Barton. "Max, Webster has an idea."

Max sprang to his feet. "I'm listening. Right now I'll take all the suggestions you've got."

"W-we need a second line of defense," Webster whispered. "I thought maybe something a bit like, well, um, like what *I* do . . ."

"Spit it out, Webster!" Spike gave his spider friend a helpful pat on the back that nearly flattened him.

"An underground trap!" Webster gasped.

Patiently, Max listened as Webster explained his idea. He thought a group of bugs should wait underground, beyond the

wall. Webster himself liked to lurk underground in his burrow, so he knew it was an
effective tactic.

"That way, any lizard who makes it over
the ramparts will run straight into our
trap!" he finished.

"That's a great idea!" Max said. "Which
bugs should we have wait in the underground burrows?"

Max spoke to Scuttler, and between them
they decided that bullet ants would be a
good choice for the underground trap. They
were fierce warriors with powerful, painful stings—which was where the name
came from. Being stung by one was like
being shot!

Suddenly it began to feel like the plan was coming together. *This might actually work*, Max thought with a grin.

Hours later, Max found Jet inspecting the fortifications. The black widow was watching the bullet ants that were burying themselves in the ground, digging down next to the half-built wall.

"I don't like it," she snapped.

"You don't like *anything*," grumbled Spike.

Max rolled his eyes at the grumpy black widow. "What are you worried about?"

"If any of the lizards get through, we'll be completely exposed. I'm not sure this

is how we should be spending our pre-battle time."

Max looked down to where Scuttler and the others were hard at work. The wall was taking shape. Termite mounds were rising up like fence posts and the wasps and hornets were busily filling the space between them with nest-like papery stuff. Scuttler waved his antennae in greeting and Max waved back.

"The head of defense seems happy," he told Jet.

Jet glowered at him.

Spike tapped Max on the shoulder. "Wow, my legs are stiff. I could use a walk. Want to come with me?"

Max followed Spike up the beach, away from Jet. "I don't really have stiff legs," Spike whispered. "I just wanted a quick word."

"I thought so." Max smiled. "What's on your mind?"

"Something's just not right." Spike settled himself down into the sand.

"What do you mean?" Max asked.

"I'm not exactly sure. But somehow the lizards are smarter than ever. They seem to know what we're up to even before we do!"

Max rubbed his chin, thinking. He glanced over his shoulder at the construction site, and at the hunched figure of Jet, who was silently watching the bugs work.

"I don't know about you, Spike, but I think we might have a bad bug in our ranks."

Spike flexed his stinger and nodded.

TRAITOR?

Time was running out. As the crimson sun set over the beach, Max stood and looked up and down the length of the newly built defenses. Mantis sentries stood in place at the towers, and bombardier beetles trooped up and down the connecting walls.

Although he couldn't see them, Max knew the secret ambush force of bullet ants was waiting under the sand just beyond the wall. If an enemy lizard somehow made it over— or through—the defenses, the bullet ants would rush up and overwhelm them.

"Fantastic work, everybug," he called out. "Now get some rest—we have a lot of work ahead."

Max went to join Barton and the other commanders in the sentry towers. Inside were little tunnels that led up to a platform in the middle. Max scrambled up and onto a ledge. It gave him and the bugs a spectacular view of the beach and the lava bridge.

"I'm impressed," Scuttler said. "These defenses ought to stop any reptile invaders in their tracks the moment they step onto Bug Island."

"Don't count your grubs before they're hatched," Jet warned.

"Aw, come on, give Max some credit!" Spike snapped. "This wall is so big and strong that even Komodo himself couldn't break through."

Jet was silent. Max turned to look out at Reptile Island, wondering when the first of the lizards would come.

Then he leaped to his feet. Something was creeping across the lava bridge *right now*. It was a lizard—and a big one!

"Incoming!" he yelled, pointing.

"Looks like we'll be putting Max's defenses to the test right now," Jet said.

"Everyone to their battle stations!" Barton roared.

The bugs sprang into action, readying their stingers and claws. Bombardier beetles primed their explosive blasts and aimed at the oncoming lizard. *Now the lizards will see how good our defenses really are,* thought Max. *This guy doesn't know what he's getting himself into . . .*

"Is it Komodo?" Spike squinted through the gathering darkness, trying to see.

"No," said Glower, the firefly intelligence specialist. "It's a desert monitor lizard. Probably Komodo's second-in-command, Lothar."

"He's on his own. Is he here to discuss terms? A treaty?" Buzz wondered.

"I doubt it," Barton said. "Lothar is as tough as they come."

Max patted the hard, compact mud of the wall. "I don't care how tough he is. He'll never get over the ramparts," he told the bugs confidently.

Steadily, Lothar approached. He was a sleek lizard with a long tail, almost as large as Komodo. He slithered from the lava bridge onto the sand of the beach, glanced up at the wall, and grinned.

"Well, look what we have here. You went and built yourselves a wall, right across the beach." His long tongue flicked out, mockingly. "Wouldn't it be a shame if something happened to it?"

Max was about to yell at Lothar that he was only one lizard, and he didn't have a hope of getting over the wall. But then he saw how worried Barton looked. He wondered if he'd overlooked something.

In the next second, Lothar threw himself into a frenzy of digging. His powerful claws flung up huge amounts of sand. His entire body vanished under the beach. All anyone could see of him was a sandy hump showing where he was burrowing . . . and that he was heading straight for the wall.

Max's mouth fell open. *Of course.* Desert monitor lizards were *burrowers*.

Panicked buzzing and clicking sounds came from the bugs guarding the wall section to his left. It was quivering, and the sand below it was shaking.

"He's breaking up the wall!" Max said in horror.

Sure enough, the wall suddenly sagged in the middle and giant chunks of papery material broke away. Beetles tumbled from their guard posts and landed on their backs, wiggling their legs helplessly in the air. Once the wall was half collapsed, the sand around the next section began to shift, too.

"They've sent the perfect reptile to sabotage our defenses!" Max raged. "They knew exactly what to do to get the better of us!"

"We've still got the bullet ants," Webster whispered.

"Are you sure about that?" Jet snarled.

On the near side of the wall, the bullet ants came scuttling out of the ground, fleeing in a mad panic. They hadn't expected to be attacked from below.

Lothar's head burst from the sand. His jaws were wide open and he was laughing. He turned and looked right at Max.

"That wall of yours didn't last long," the lizard mocked. "Hope you didn't waste too much time building it."

"Battle Bugs, attack!" Barton yelled. "Take him down!"

"I don't think so," Lothar gloated. He twisted around so he could vanish back into the tunnel he'd dug under the sand. "Good luck when the rest of my forces arrive! You'll need it, without your precious defenses!"

Laughing, the lizard dived back into his tunnel.

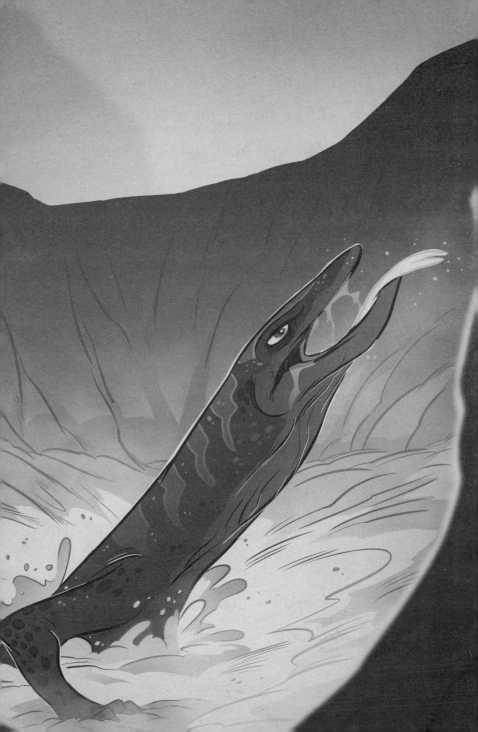

"There he goes!" Barton and the other bugs tried to follow him, eager for a fight, as he disappeared back under the sand and toward the lava bridge.

Max was about to go after them, too, but a lean black spider leg held him back.

"You need to follow me," Jet said.

"What?" Max asked, eager to join the fight.

"Lothar won't go straight back to the lava bridge. He's too cunning. I think I know where we can ambush him."

Max hesitated for a moment. "Okay. Let me just tell Spike first."

"No time for that," Jet urged. "We have to move, *now!*"

Max looked on as the other bugs quickly burrowed under the sand in hot pursuit of the lizard. *Maybe she's right*, he thought. *Maybe we can head him off.*

"Okay, let's do it," he said. "Where to?"

"This way," Jet said. "Follow me."

The black widow led Max away from the bug fortifications and up toward the jungle on the edge of the beach. They ran swiftly up the sand dunes and over the ridge, until lush green foliage and brightly colored flowers dwarfed Max all around.

"How much farther?" Max complained after they'd trudged through the jungle for what felt like ages. The light was beginning to dim in the sky, and already the beach was well out of sight.

"Only a little ways now," Jet assured him. "We're almost there."

"You said that five minutes ago! And there's been no sign of Lothar." Suddenly, a sinister thought crossed Max's mind. "We're not going after the lizard at all, are we?"

"No, we are not." Jet spun around to face him. Her eyes glittered in the gathering darkness. She had a hungry look on her face.

"What's going on?" Max demanded. His heart was thumping with fear. Jet had lured him well away from any bugs that could help him now.

"You know very well, traitor!" Jet hissed.

Max's blood ran cold. How could she think such a thing? "I'm not a traitor!"

"Don't bother denying it!" Before Max could try and reason with her, Jet had rushed forward, knocking him to the ground. She rested one hairy spider leg on his chest and bared her fangs.

"Everything you've done to defend us has failed," she said. "The lizards avoided your trip wires and they knew just how to destroy our wall. There is a lizard spy in our midst and I know that it's you, human. You're not one of us!"

"That's not true!" Max protested. "I'm on the Battle Bugs' side. Ask Barton!"

Jet's eyes glittered. "For you, the bug war is over."

THE INVASION BEGINS

Max groggily opened his eyes. He tried to move his arms and legs, but they were held fast. He peered down and saw he was wrapped in a tight cocoon of sticky spider webbing. His cocoon swayed back and forth, suspended from a high branch in a tree. Suddenly he felt dizzy.

As the sun steadily rose across the bay,

dark thoughts began to race through Max's mind. *It's not my fault that the lizards knew all about the defenses!* he thought sourly. *But Jet was right about one thing: The Battle Bugs have a traitor.*

Off in the distance he could still see the volcano, the Great Reptilicus, bellowing out dark smoke. Even from this far away, he could hear loud rumbling noises. The volcano was clearly about to erupt, just as the elder turtles had predicted.

Suddenly, as he peered out across the bay, an even more terrifying sight confronted Max. Row after row of lizards, of all shapes and sizes, were slowly making their way across the lava bridge.

"No!" he yelled, struggling against his

webbing bonds. "They've already started the invasion!"

He could just make out the lizards crashing into the waiting ranks of the beach bug army. Scorpions, spiders, beetles, and even flies battered away at the invaders. For now, the sheer mass of bugs was keeping the lizards from advancing too far inland, but it was obvious the bug ranks wouldn't hold forever.

"I've got to get down there and help!" Max yelled as he thrashed around, bouncing on the end of the webbing line. Being human was supposed to give him advantages the bugs didn't have! If only he had something that could cut the web. Some human tool . . .

Wait. He thought. *I do have something.*

Max angled his hand into his front jeans pocket. With a flick of his wrist, his fingers closed around the rubber grip of the screwdriver he'd put back in his pocket at the science fair.

He slid the screwdriver out of his pocket and grasped it like a dagger. He dragged it up against the webbing covering his chest. The sharp metal began to cut away some of the webbing. Spider silk may have been able to hold more weight than steel, but luckily it was much easier to cut through.

"So much for Jet thinking us non-bugs were useless," Max cried. He was trying to free his arm when a crash from below grabbed his attention.

Like a black-and-orange vision from his

worst nightmare, the Gila monster was back. And it looked hungry.

Max froze.

"Well, well," it said, licking its scaly lips. "The bugs have left me a snack, before the banquet begins. And it's the very one I was sent to eat yesterday!"

So the lizards are *after me,* Max thought. *But why?*

Even though he was dangling from a branch, Max knew he wasn't out of the reptile's reach. It lunged up at him, jaws wide. Max frantically tried to swing out of the way, but the Gila monster's jaws clamped shut on the cocoon.

The Gila monster tugged, and Max was torn down from the branch. Jaws coated in

venomous saliva were pressing against his body. Jet's webbing was the only thing protecting him now. Fortunately, the fall had torn the webbing, freeing his arm.

"Take that!" Max yelled, swiping at the lizard. He gripped the screwdriver tightly and jammed it into the reptile's nostril. With a roar of pain, the Gila monster flung its head back. Max went flying out of its jaws and landed in a patch of grass.

Max had to get free. He ripped and slashed with the screwdriver, but his legs were still all tangled up.

"I didn't know human beings had stingers," the Gila monster grunted. "That stinger won't do you any good, though. I'm still going to eat you!"

Max readied his screwdriver as the Gila monster opened its mouth and lunged.

"GET AWAY FROM HIM!"

Spike came charging out from between the trees and jammed his stinger into the Gila monster's underbelly, making it howl with pain. Before it could turn to attack the scorpion, Spike had grabbed hold of its foreleg with his pincers and held fast.

"THAT'S WHAT YOU GET FOR TRYING TO EAT MY FRIEND!" Spike yelled.

"Let me go!" the Gila monster wailed.

With a sudden surge of strength, the reptile pulled out of Spike's grasp and went galloping off toward the lava bridge.

Spike waved his pincers in the air as it retreated. "Tell your boss he can expect the same treatment! Bug Island isn't his, and it never will be!"

"Thanks, Spike." Max said, quickly freeing himself from the last of the webbing. "I thought I was a goner for sure."

"I'm just glad you're safe, little buddy. I've been looking for you all night . . ." Spike trailed off as he picked up a ragged scrap of Max's cocoon. "Wait a minute—this is spider silk!" he cried. "Who did this to you?" he asked, his voice shaking with anger.

"It was Jet," Max said. "She called me a traitor."

"What?" Spike opened and closed his pincers. "She's the traitor, wrapping you up like this! She probably told that monster lizard where to find you, too. She won't get away with it. We've got to tell Barton. She's got to face Battle Bug justice!"

"We will tell Barton," Max said sternly. "But first, we've got a battle to fight. And a war to win."

Max climbed onto Spike's back. Together, the two of them rode toward the beach.

It was time to decide the final fate of Bug Island, once and for all.

BACK TO THE BEACH

The bugs at the back of the army cheered as they saw Max and Spike coming toward them.

"We thought you'd been eaten," a mantis chirped.

"Not today," Max said. "Let me through, bugs. I need to get to the front."

Spike pushed through the eager bugs and climbed a rock so that Max could get a good view of the beach. He shielded his eyes from the bright morning sun and looked out at the battle.

The bugs had formed a massive defensive line, making the most of what was left of the wall. Spiders, centipedes, and termites scuttled in every direction, trying to find where they were needed most.

Lizards crowded all along the lava bridge, nose to tail, from one island's shore to the other. The evacuation of Reptile Island was well underway. But with so many of them all trying to leave at once, they couldn't move very fast. It was like rush hour on a city highway.

That could work in our favor, Max thought.

At the bugs' end of the beach, reptile warriors were scrambling off the lava bridge and into the fight as fast as they could. Komodo had sent some of his heaviest units in first: quick-darting salamanders, thick-skinned thorny devil lizards, slithering coral snakes, geckos, chameleons, and gliding lizards. There were more lizards than Max had ever seen before.

Buzz and her hornet squadron swept past overhead and plunged down to deliver a barrage of stings before roaring up into the air again.

"Come on!" Max yelled to Spike. "We're needed!"

The scorpion galloped forward, carrying Max through to the front line.

All of the bug battalions were there, including the spider squadrons, the mantis strike force, the all-important bombardier beetle brigades, and the most numerous soldiers of all, the army ants.

"Hit them from both sides," Max yelled. "Don't let them get off the bridge! Attack!"

The two flanks of the bug army thundered into the fray. From above, the bug forces would look like a pair of scissors snapping shut on the lizards.

Classic pincer move, Max thought with satisfaction.

Barton flew past overhead, and zeroed in to land right by Max. A hissing lizard lunged, but Barton grabbed it just in time and tossed it back where it had come from.

"Max! Where have you been?"

"It's a long story, General. I'll have to explain later." He jerked a thumb at the oncoming reptile forces. "Should we deal with this little problem first?"

"Sounds like a good idea to me," Barton rumbled.

Side by side, they prepared for the final onslaught.

Max pointed to the lava bridge, where a gigantic dragon-like figure was barging through the reptile ranks in his haste to reach the bugs. Some lizards were knocked into the water and started flailing around, unable to swim.

"Look, Komodo's coming," Max said.

Barton flexed his mandibles. "Let him come. It's time to finish this, once and for all." He paused and looked around him. "It's been an honor to fight by your side, my friend."

"Same here," Max said.

Barton opened his wing case and hovered in the air. "On my command . . . Battle Bugs, *charge*!"

The giant centipede legions, led by Gigantus, charged into the fight. Behind them came the swarming millipedes, and the bullet ants. The skies filled with the fury of the hornets, with Buzz out in front. Wasps and bees came sweeping through alongside them.

Pincers slashed, claws grabbed, and sting after sting found its mark. They were fighting not just for their lives, but also for their home. Max lost track of time in the chaos. The noise was unbelievable, with the hisses and croaks of wounded lizards mingling with the furious buzzes and screeches of the bugs. He directed Spike to attack one opponent, then another, always striking where the lizards were weakest.

At one point, Spike seemed tired, and so Max urged him forward. "Come on, buddy! Don't give up now!"

"Give up?" Spike roared. "Never!" He reared forward and slammed his pincers down on the heads of two attacking lizards.

Still the lizards came. Max realized the

bugs were slowly, but surely, being pushed back. The more ground the bugs yielded, the more lizards could swarm off the lava bridge and onto the beach.

They're winning, he thought.

"Lizards, cease fighting! Hold your ground!" roared the voice of General Komodo. He came triumphantly swaggering up to the front, while his exhausted troops paused in their onslaught.

The bug forces stood braced, waiting for the fighting to begin again. Barton picked his way through to the front of the bug ranks. With each of their forces behind them, primed to fight, Barton and Komodo stared each other down.

"Was this the best you could do, Barton?"

Komodo sighed. "A few measly trip wires, a half-built wall, and an ant buffet?"

"Bug Island will never be yours," Barton retorted.

"It won't be Bug Island for much longer!" Komodo roared with laughter. "I hereby name this place New Reptile Island. A fitting home for my people, complete with all the bugs we could ever eat."

"You think it will be that easy?" Barton yelled. "Even if you occupy our island, we'll never give up the fight."

Komodo slowly shook his head, his tongue flickering all the while. "I doubt that," he snarled, a smile creeping across his lips. "One of your bugs has already seen sense and come over to our side."

"What?" Barton snarled. "You're lying!"

"We've had an agent on your side all along, passing information to us!" Komodo gloated. "How else do you think we knew about your defenses?"

I knew it, Max thought. *That traitorous spider, Jet! She's been working for Komodo all along. No wonder she tried to imprison me on the day of the battle.*

He looked across to the spider battalion, where Jet was glaring back at him. But to Max's amazement, it wasn't Jet who stepped forward.

It was Barton's handpicked commander of defense. The golden-green scarab beetle, Scuttler!

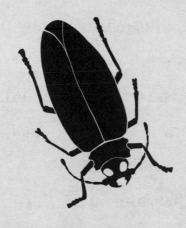

BARTON VS. KOMODO

Before the startled bugs could stop him, Scuttler opened his wing case and launched himself into the air. He flew over the reptile front ranks, reached Komodo, and settled on his shoulder.

"Meet your new ruler, bugs," said Komodo. "King Scuttler the First. He will keep you in line, meek and obedient to your reptile masters."

"*He* was the traitor?" Max cried.

"Scuttler!" Barton boomed. "Why? I thought you were loyal."

"You didn't think at all, Barton!" Scuttler snarled. "You let the human do all your thinking for you. You aren't fit to lead the bugs—but I am!"

"You?" Barton repeated.

"I am a golden scarab, not some common beetle like you," Scuttler said. We are *royal*. Born to rule! It is my destiny to replace you."

"Is that really what you want, Scuttler? To rule over an island of enslaved bugs, as General Komodo's puppet? Are you *that* desperate to be a king?"

"It is what I deserve," Scuttler said, pompously.

Max saw Jet give him an apologetic glance. He gave her one in return. They'd both thought the other was the traitor, when the real traitor had been right under their noses the whole time.

"You will never rule us," Barton said savagely. "I will fight to the death to save Bug Island!"

"Me, too," yelled Spike.

"And me," said Webster and Buzz.

Max glared at Komodo. "And me."

"Perhaps we should put your commitment to the test," Komodo said.

"AS YOU WISH!" With a mighty battle cry, Barton flew right at Komodo's face.

Bugs and lizards alike scattered out of the way as the two generals lunged at each other. A hatred that had lasted longer than anyone could remember finally burst out in full force.

Barton hovered and struck with his huge mandibles, jabbing at Komodo's eyes. Komodo snapped with his jaws, trying to tear Barton out of the sky. For a huge beetle, Barton was surprisingly fast.

Komodo tried to swipe with a claw, but Barton dodged at the last second. Scuttler cowered, still clinging to Komodo's shoulder. Barton flew up behind Komodo's head, forcing the reptile leader to twist and turn angrily. "Stay still! Let me finish you!"

Barton grabbed Komodo's face. He dug his mandibles in deep, making the general yell. Komodo raked with his claws, but couldn't reach the titan beetle. His legs were just too stubby.

A cheer went up from the bug ranks. Suddenly, it seemed they had hope again.

A distant rumble reached Max's ears. The volcano was near eruption, but all eyes were watching the generals fight. He turned to look and saw something that almost stopped his heart.

Just like Steve's soda volcano had, this one was about to break apart from the force of the eruption. There were cracks running down the side.

By the look of it, when the volcano blew, tons of rock would break loose and plunge into the sea. *The eruption is going to be just like the soda volcano back at the science fair. Only a lot bigger.* Max glanced from the bugs to the volcano and back, and knew what he had to do.

"Battle Bugs, surge forward!" he shouted.

While Komodo howled and screamed and tried to shake Barton off, the bugs stampeded forward, plunging into the lizard ranks. The lizards, startled by the bugs' fury, staggered backward.

"Keep going!" Max yelled. "We've got to fight them back onto the lava bridge!"

"What you got in mind, buddy?" grunted

Spike as he flung an attacking lizard back at its own forces, sending lizards flying.

"If we can trap them on the lava bridge, then we've as good as won," Max said. "Look!"

Max pointed at the volcano, which was belching out alarming amounts of smoke. A violent rumble shook the earth, as if the whole world were being torn in half. Lava sprayed from the volcano crater.

Then, just as an orange fountain of lava shot up into the air, the whole side of the volcano collapsed.

The destruction seemed to happen in slow motion. Thousands of tons of rock went tumbling toward the water.

"Oh," said Spike hollowly. "I see what you mean."

With a thunderous *KATHOOM*, the rocks plunged into the ocean between the two islands.

Half a mountain collapsing into the sea all at once was going to displace a lot of water. First, a white geyser blasted up.

Next came the tsunami.

Max and Spike stared in awe as a wall of water as high as a house came rushing toward them . . .

LAST BATTLE

"One last push!" Max yelled. "We have to drive them back over the bridge. Go, go, go!"

The Battle Bugs piled in, from the biggest to the smallest, shoving the lizards back in one final desperate moment. As well as the warrior bugs, the little worker termites and the ladybugs and dragonflies joined the charge. Spiders linked arms with ants. Hornets and butterflies flew into battle together. Not one bug was left out.

Faced with the overwhelming power of the bug forces advancing as one, the lizards could only retreat. They staggered back across the sandy beach onto the lava bridge. Thousands of angry claws, mandibles, and stingers held them at bay.

"Regroup!" Komodo roared, still trying to throw off Barton. "What are you scared of? They're just bugs!"

Max rode Spike at the head of the bug charge. Momentum carried him forward. All around him, bugs were yelling their battle cries. They rushed onto the lava bridge, driving the lizards before them. They couldn't stop now. The lizard forces were in complete disarray. They were rapidly return-ing to Reptile Island, even though volcanic debris still rained down.

Max glanced across the glittering sea. The tsunami was coming. It raced toward the lava bridge, so high it almost crested the vol-cano. Most of the lizards were huddled on the far shore of Reptile Island.

"That's far enough," Max shouted to the bugs. "Back to Bug Island!"

General Komodo snarled down at Max as he and Spike galloped back across the lava bridge. "So, human. You turn around and run, when you could face me? You are a coward after all." Komodo, distracted by Barton, seemed not to notice that most of his army had deserted him.

Barton let go of Komodo's head, flew up into the air above him, and laughed.

"You dare laugh at me in my moment of triumph?" Komodo growled.

"We're not running from you. We're running from THAT." Max cried over his shoulder.

A shadow fell across Komodo.

"General! Look out!" Scuttler squealed, still clinging to Komodo's shoulder.

"What?" In genuine confusion, Komodo turned to look.

Looming above him was the towering wave, churning and sloshing, so high that it blocked out the sun. Komodo's eyes bugged almost out of his skull and his mouth gaped in a despairing wail: *"Noooo!"*

Spike charged up the beach and carried Max to safety. The last few bugs that had been on the beach scrambled to higher ground. Barton flew as fast as he could alongside the roaring wall of water.

Komodo tried to sprint across the bridge to Bug Island, but he wasn't fast enough.

The wave struck. The world was blotted out in a fury of roaring water and surging white foam. Max saw Komodo himself go under, with Scuttler still clinging hopelessly to him. They rode the top of the wave and disappeared out of sight around the far side of the island.

Slowly, the current died away and the water receded. Max and the bugs stared in amazement at the remains of the lava

bridge. It had been more fragile than they knew. The enormous wave had smashed the middle part of it completely away.

"Barton!" Max jumped off Spike and ran down to the water's edge, where Barton had washed ashore.

Barton's wings were waterlogged and one of his antennae looked crooked. The wave had knocked into him. Spike, Jet, and the others all crowded around him.

"What are you all doing?" Barton asked, struggling to his feet and coughing up water. "You didn't think I was a goner, did you? It'll take more than a splash of water to finish this old bug off!"

*　　*　　*

Later, Max and a dried-off Barton stood on top of the remains of one of the termites' beach towers. Max looked out at the ruins of the Great Reptilicus. He was sorry to go, but knew he'd soon be missed at school if he stayed much longer.

Webster, Jet, Glower, Buzz, and Spike stood nearby, almost glowing with pride. Below them, across the beach, the bugs of Bug Island had gathered to say farewell to Max, their hero. Hundreds of thousands of multifaceted eyes looked silently up at him.

"I trusted Max to help us win the day," Barton said. "But I never expected he would make Bug Island safe forever. Now that the lava bridge has been destroyed, the lizard army can never reach us again."

"You may not be a bug," Jet added, "but from one warrior to another, I'm glad you're on our side." She shook his hand with one of her legs.

Max hugged Barton, Webster, Buzz, and lastly Spike, who seemed a little sad. "Look after yourself, buddy," he said. "And come back anytime!"

"You will always have a hero's welcome here," Barton added. "And to make sure that Bug Island always remembers the human who saved us . . ." He pointed to the cliff, where the termites had been hard at work. A lumpy but still recognizable statue of Max, made from mud and dung, stood out-lined against the sky. Max grinned.

"I'll miss all of you," he said. "Good-bye, Battle Bugs." Max lifted his magnifying glass up to the sky. "Never leave a bug behind!" he called, as he was sucked up into the sky. Max got one last look at his bug friends waving up at him, and then the world began spinning around him, faster and faster.

Max found himself alone in the classroom, with his encyclopedia still open on the desk. He closed it and tucked it into his backpack, feeling a little sad. Now that his friends were safe, would he ever be able to return to Bug Island again?

With a sigh, Max headed back to the school gym. At least he still had his ant farm to look after, not to mention all the cool bugs he could find over vacation.

Steve met him at the door. "Max! Where have you been? They're just about to announce the big winner! Debbie DeSantos came in second with that solar system thing, can you believe it?"

"I . . . I guess not," Max said, his head still whirring from the trip to Bug Island.

He looked up to see Principal Marsh standing at a podium. His voice rang out across the gym hall. "Finally, it gives me great pleasure to announce that first prize . . ."

"C'mon, soda volcano!" Steve jokingly whispered.

". . . goes to Max Darwin," the principal finished. "For The World of Ants!"

Max beamed. First he'd helped save Bug Island, then he won first prize in the science fair. *Not bad for one day!* he thought.

Max crossed the hall and went to shake the principal's hand, while applause rang out around him.

"I have seen many ant farms before," the principal said as he leaned in. "But there was something different about how you constructed and presented yours."

"What was that?" Max asked.

"You recognized that the ants were living creatures, not just test subjects. You spoke of them not just with knowledge, but compassion."

"Thanks," Max said as he accepted the small trophy.

As he climbed off the stage, Steve slapped him on the back and grinned. "Congrats! I guess the best project won."

"Thanks, Steve. Want to come bug hunting later?"

"Somehow, I thought you might ask that." Steve rolled his eyes. "Sure. Meet you in the park at five. Bring your big bug book."

Max smiled. *If only you knew what that book could really do.*

He opened up his backpack to pack away his things, and took a fond look at the encyclopedia.

Suddenly, his heart skipped a beat.

Deep in the shadows of his backpack, the encyclopedia's pages glowed with a faint, but unmistakable, silver light, before going dark again.

Max's smile grew broader.

Maybe I'll see the Battle Bugs again soon . . .

REAL LIFE
BATTLE BUGS!

Black widow spider

The females of this species have jet-black bodies with distinctive, bright-red, hourglass-shaped markings on their abdomens. They're much more recognizable than the smaller, gray/brown males—and they're much more deadly.

The black widow spider is also highly venomous and dangerous to humans. The spider's bite can be as much as fifteen times stronger than a rattlesnake's and can cause nausea, muscle pain, and difficulty breathing.

Fortunately, black widow attacks are rare. They only bite humans in self-defense, or if you make the mistake of sitting on one. So, if you find yourself in a location with a black widow presence, it might be best to check before you sit down!

Scarab beetle

The family of beetles known as Scarabaeidae consists of a massive thirty thousand different species. The largest species, and most widely known among them, are the scarab beetles.

The most famous of the scarab beetles is the *Scarabaeus sacer.* This particular insect was sacred to the ancient Egyptians and it represented creation and rebirth. The way that the beetles roll huge balls of dung across the ground mirrored the Egyptians' belief in the sun god, who would roll the sun across the sky each morning.

The scarab is one of many coprophagous species of insect. This means that it feeds on the waste products of other living things. Female beetles lay their eggs in the center of dung balls. When the young are ready to hatch, they have a meal ready and waiting for them!

READ MAX'S FIRST ADVENTURE WITH THE BATTLE BUGS!

LIZARD ATTACK!

The lizard's tongue shot from its mouth like a whip. Then, slowly, it lumbered forward. Max held his breath. It was gigantic. The ground shook with every stamp of its big, clawed feet.

"How nice of you to drop in," it hissed, "just in time for dinner."

Max gulped. From where he was sitting,

the lizard looked as big as a dinosaur. It could easily win a battle against the scorpion. As for the tiny human being on its back . . .

"Back off, you scaly bully," said the scorpion. It raised its stinger threateningly, ready to strike. The stinger's pointed tip was hanging right next to Max's head, a bead of white venom on the end. Max edged away from it, lying down as flat as he could and peering over the scorpion's eyes.

The lizard hissed. "I don't like it when my snacks fight back," it spat. It advanced again, backing the scorpion up against the branch they'd just climbed.

Max knew that the emperor scorpion was well armed. Its huge, powerful pincers and venomous stinger made it a dangerous enemy. But the lizard's scaly skin would be far too thick and tough for the scorpion's stinger to pierce.

There has to be some *way out of this,* Max thought, his heart pounding. *Maybe the scorpion can outrun it?* He looked at the lizard's powerful legs, and swallowed hard. Scorpions could run fast, but the alligator lizard looked quick, too, and it wasn't carrying a passenger.

The lizard opened its mouth, showing its sharp, pointed teeth, and suddenly leaped forward. Max clung on tightly as the scorpion scuttled to the side, dodging out of the lizard's reach.

The lizard turned slowly to face them, its yellow eyes glittering. Once again, it stepped closer. Then it stopped and tipped its head to one side.

"What do you have on your back?" it asked curiously.

Max looked up to see that the lizard was staring straight at him. The scales on its flat, crocodile-like head were all the same size, except around its nostrils, where they were smaller and darker. Suddenly, Max remembered something.

"Quick!" he whispered to the scorpion. "His scales are weaker around his nostrils! Use your pincers there!"

"Stop that whispering!" bellowed the lizard. "What sort of thing are you, anyway?"

Max glared back at the lizard. "I'm his secret weapon!" he shouted.

And with that the scorpion darted forward, taking the reptile by surprise. Before it could react, the scorpion snapped one of its pincers onto the lizard's nose. The lizard gave a high-pitched hiss and backed away, twisting its head in pain.

"Let's go!" shouted Max.

The scorpion charged around the lizard as it retreated, holding a clawed foot to its injured snout. But Max knew they weren't out of danger yet. The lizard might still come after them. And if it did, it would be even angrier than before.

The scorpion seemed to have realized this, too, because it was running as fast as its legs could carry it. "Thanks for the tip," it shouted back to Max.

JOIN THE RACE!

It's an incredible adventure through the animal kingdom, as kids zip-line, kayak, and scuba dive their way to the finish line! Packed with cool facts about amazing creatures, dangerous habitats, and more!

■ SCHOLASTIC

scholastic.com

RA

MEET RANGER

A time–traveling golden retriever with search-and-rescue training . . . and a nose for danger!